God
Has A Sense
Of Humor
For Heaven's Sake

A Collection of Religious Humor

God Bless You

M Chamberlin 2010

Mike Chamberlin

Outskirts Press, Inc.
Denver, Colorado

Outskirts Press, Inc.
http://www.outskirtspress.com

ISBN: 978-1-4327-4352-9

Outskirts Press and the "OP" logo are trademarks belonging to Outskirts Press, Inc.

PRINTED IN THE UNITED STATES OF AMERICA

FOREWORD

I made my living on the evening news. I was a TV Anchorman who spent a lifetime working strange hours and relying on coffee to get me through the day and night. Like all of you I have my favorite Starbucks and found a path to it twice a day. The path that led from my TV station to the barista went right by a very creative church. Every week they would place a very clever, if not funny message on the outside marquee or billboard. Every week I looked forward to seeing the new slogan. After years of driving by the church, I finally stopped in to meet the person responsible. She told me the congregation had even become involved in the mission of the message. She had been keeping all the slogans in a file. I convinced her to release the file to me, and I would see the messages became part of a bigger project...a book! So she turned over the file and one thing led to another. In addition to my broadcasting, I was also a singer. I have performed at countless worship services, and heard a lot of jokes from ministers along the way. Many I have written down, others just found their way to me as I started researching this book. The book begins with many of the "signs" I drove by. The rest of the book is a collection of His humor. I have built this book to be shared by families. How fun would it be to sit with the family and share some of these funny stories? In the pages of this book is proof that God truly does have a sense of humor, I mean if he didn't how could you explain the platypus? Enjoy, as you laugh with the Lord.

Mike Chamberlin

SIGNS

IF YOU'RE LOOKING FOR A SIGN TO GET BACK TO CHURCH... THIS IS IT!

GOD

ANSWERS

KNEE-MAIL

STOP, DROP
AND ROLL
WILL NOT
WORK
IN HELL

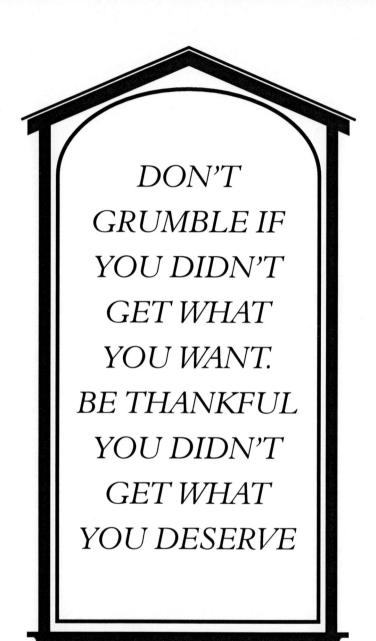

DON'T GRUMBLE IF YOU DIDN'T GET WHAT YOU WANT. BE THANKFUL YOU DIDN'T GET WHAT YOU DESERVE

GIVE SATAN
AN INCH AND
HE'LL BE A
RULER

YOU THINK
IT'S HOT HERE?

–GOD

EASTER
SHOULD BE
MORE THAN
SOMETHING
TO DYE FOR

WE NEED
TO TALK

−GOD

*SPEAK WELL
OF YOUR
ENEMIES.
AFTER ALL,
YOU MADE
THEM*

LET'S MEET AT MY HOUSE SUNDAY BEFORE THE GAME

– GOD

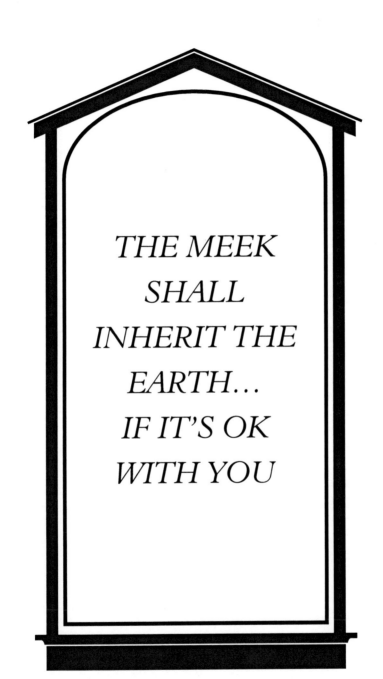

*THE MEEK
SHALL
INHERIT THE
EARTH…
IF IT'S OK
WITH YOU*

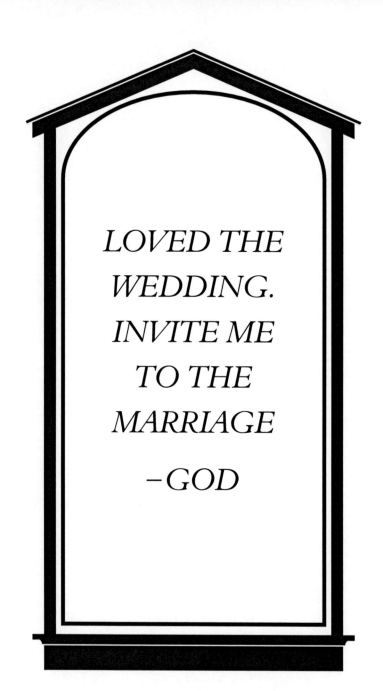

LOVED THE WEDDING. INVITE ME TO THE MARRIAGE

–GOD

GOD IS
PERFECT…
ONLY MAN
MAKES
MISTEAKS

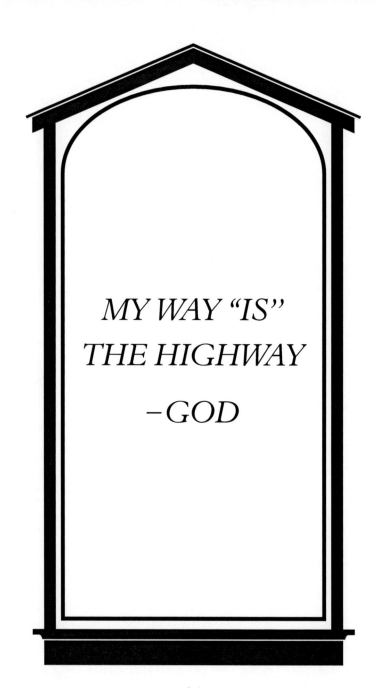

MY WAY "IS" THE HIGHWAY

–GOD

OUR CHURCH
IS PRAYER
CONDITIONED

DON'T MAKE
ME COME
DOWN THERE

–GOD

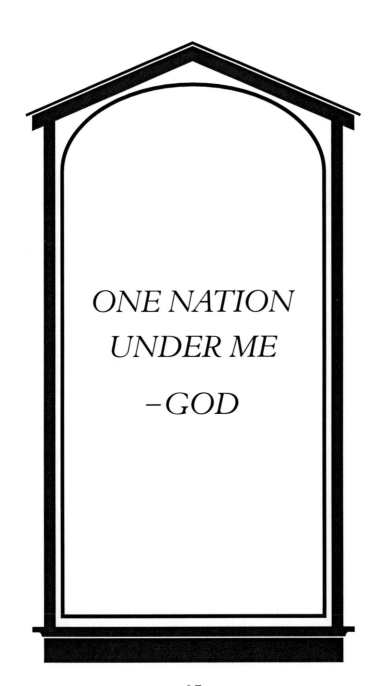

ONE NATION
UNDER ME
–GOD

READ THE
BIBLE.
IT WILL SCARE
THE HELL OUT
OF YOU

IF GOD HAD A
REFRIGERATOR,
YOUR PICTURE
WOULD BE
ON IT

TRY OUR SUNDAYS. THEY'RE BETTER THAN BASKIN ROBBINS

SEVEN DAYS WITHOUT PRAYER MAKES ONE WEAK

THE JOKES

ALL IN A DAYS WORK

God: "Whew!" I just created a 24 hour period of alternating light and darkness on earth."

Angel: "What are you going to do now?"

God: "Call it a day."

THE TRUTH HURTS

"I hope you didn't take it personally, Reverend," an embarrassed woman said after a church service, "when my husband walked out during your sermon."

"I did find it rather disconcerting," the preacher replied.

"It's not a reflection on you sir," insisted the churchgoer, "Ralph has been walking in his sleep ever since he was a child."

AN AXE OF GOD

An elderly woman had just returned to her home from an evening of religious service when an intruder startled her. As she caught the man in the act of robbing her home of its valuables she yelled, "Stop! Acts 2:38." (…Turn from your sin…)

The burglar stopped dead in his tracks. The woman calmly called the police and explained what she had done. As the officer cuffed the man to take him in, he asked the burglar, "Why did you just stand there? All the old lady did was yell scripture at you."

"Scripture?" replied the burglar, "she said she had an AXE and two 38's!"

HYMN/HIM

A pastor explained to the congregation that the church was in need of some extra money, so he asked them to consider being more than generous. He offered whoever gave the most would be able to pick three hymns. After the plate was passed he found someone had graciously offered a $1,000 bill. He asked the person to stand up, much to his amazement an 85-year-old woman rose. He thanked her and said, "You may now pick three hymns. " She said fine and looked over the congregation, found three handsome men and said, "I'll take him, him and him!"

One Sunday morning, the priest noticed little Johnny staring up at the large plaque that hung in the foyer of the church. It was covered with names, and small American flags were mounted on either side of it. The seven year old had been staring at the plaque for some time, so the priest walked up, stood beside the boy and said quietly, "Good morning, Johnny."

"Good morning, Father," replied the young man still focused on the plaque. "Father Scott, what is this?" Little Johnny asked. "Well son, it's a memorial to all the men and women who died in the service." Soberly they stood together for a few quiet moments when Johnny's voice was barely audible when he asked, "Which service, the 9:45 or the 11:15?"

The minister was preoccupied with the thoughts of how he was going to, at the end of the service, ask the congregation to come up with more money for church repairs. He was even more annoyed to find the regular organist was out sick and a substitute had been brought in at the last minute.

The substitute wanted to know what to play. "Here's a copy of the service," he said impatiently. "But you'll have to think of something to play after I make the announcement about the finances.

During the service, the minister paused and said, "Brothers and sisters we are in great difficulty. The roof repairs cost twice as much as we expected and we need $4,000 more. Any of you who can pledge $100 or more please stand up."

At that moment, the substitute organist played "The Star Spangled Banner."

And that is how the substitute became the regular organist!

EMAIL FROM HELL

There once was an Illinois man who left the snow-filled streets of Chicago for a vacation in Florida. His wife was on a business trip and was planning to meet him there the next day. When he reached his hotel he decided to send his wife a quick email. Unable to find the scrap of paper on which he wrote her email address, he did his best to type it from memory. Unfortunately, he missed by one letter, and his note was directed instead to an elderly preachers wife, whose husband had passed away only the day before. When the grieving widow checked her email, she took one look at the monitor and let out a piercing scream, and fainted to the floor. At the sound her family rushed into the room and saw the note on the screen: "Dearest Wife, just checked in. Everything prepared for your arrival tomorrow. Signed, Your eternally loving husband. P.S. Sure is hot down here."

A doctor, a nurse and a top executive of an HMO have died and are in line together at the Pearly Gates. St. Peter speaks with them and asks them what good they have done in their lives. The doctor says, "I have devoted my life to the sick and needy and have had a part in caring for the healing of thousands of people." St. Peter replies, "That's great go ahead into heaven." "And what about you?" The nurse states, "I have supported the doctor and his patients my entire adult life and have helped them lead healthy lives." "Wonderful. Please proceed in with the doctor." "And what about you?" The HMO executive says, "I was the president of a very large Health Maintenance organization. I was responsible for the health care of millions of people all over the country." St Peter says, "Oh, I see. Please go on in…but you can only stay for two nights!"

HIGH TITHE

There were two men shipwrecked on an island. The minute they got on the island one of them started screaming and yelling, "We're going to die! We're going to die! There's no food! There's no water! We're going to die!" The second man was perched against a palm tree and acting very calmly that it drove the first man crazy. "Don't you understand?!? We're going to die!" The second man replied, "You don't understand, I make $200,000 a week." "What difference does that make," said the dumbfounded first man. The other man replied, "I make $200,000 a week and I tithe 10% of that to my church. Trust me...my pastor will find me!"

SURELY YOU JEST

The story goes that a certain court jester went too far one day and insulted his king. The king became so infuriated that he sentenced the jester to be executed. His court preyed upon the king to have mercy on this man who had served him well for so many years. After consulting with the church leaders, the king relented only enough to give the jester his choice as to how he would like to die. True to form, the jester replied, "If it's all the same to you my lord, I'd like to die of old age!"

NO THANKS

A man was walking along when suddenly he got his foot stuck in some railroad tracks. He tried to get it out, but it was really stuck deep in the tracks. He heard the noise of the approaching train and turned to see the train within sight. He panicked and started to pray, "God, please get my foot out of these tracks and I will stop drinking." Nothing happened, it was still stuck and getting closer. He prayed again, "God please release my foot and I will stop drinking AND swearing!" Still nothing... and the train was just seconds away. One last time, "God if you get my foot out of the tracks I will quit drinking, smoking AND swearing." Suddenly his foot shot out of the tracks and he was able to dive out of the way, just as the train passed. He got up, dusted himself off, looked towards Heaven and said, "Thanks anyway God, but I got it myself."

PEACH BRANDY

A Baptist preacher went to see a member of the community and invited him to come to Church on Sunday morning. The man was a producer of fine peach brandy and told the preacher he would attend church IF the pastor would drink some brandy and admit doing so in front of the congregation. The preacher agreed and drank up.

Sunday morning came and the man came to church. The preacher recognized him from the pulpit and said: "I see Mr. Johnson is here with us this morning. I want to thank him for his hospitality this week and especially the peaches he gave me and the spirit in which they were given."

Fred was in the hospital, near death, so the family sent for the pastor. As the pastor stood beside the bed, Fred's frail condition grew worse, as he motioned frantically for something to write on. The pastor lovingly handed him a pen and paper, Fred used his last ounce of strength to scribe the note. Then he died.

The pastor thought it best not to look at then note and tucked it away in the pocket of his jacket. Several days later, at the funeral, the pastor delivered the eulogy. He realized he was wearing the same jacket as the day Fred died.

"You know," he said, "old Fred handed me a note just before he died. I haven't read it, but knowing Fred, I'm sure there's a word of inspiration there for us all."

He unfolded the note and read aloud, "You're standing on my oxygen tube!"

THE BOSS IS HERE

A Cardinal ran into the Pope's office and said, "Your Holiness, Jesus just rode into the Vatican on a donkey. What do we do?"

The Pope looked up from his work and replied, "Look busy."

OOPS

A drunken man staggers into a Catholic church and sits down in a confessional box and says nothing.

The bewildered priest coughs to attract his attention, but still the man says nothing. The priest knocks on the wall three times in a final attempt to get the man to speak.

Finally the drunk says, "No use knockin' man, there's no paper in this one either."

During a recent ecumenical gathering, a secretary rushed in shouting, "The building is on fire!!!"

The METHODISTS gathered in the corner and prayed.

The BAPTISTS cried, "Where is the holy water?"

The QUAKERS quietly praised God for the blessing the fire brings.

The LUTHERANS posted a notice on the door declaring the fire was evil.

The CATHOLICS passed the plate to cover the damage.

The JEWS posted symbols on the door, hoping the fire would pass by.

The EPISCOPALIANS formed a procession and marched out.

The PRESBYTERIANS appointed a chairperson who was to appoint a committee and look into the matter then file a written report.

The SECRETARY grabbed a fire extinguisher and put the fire out.

PREACHING

The preacher was wired for sound with a lapel microphone, and as he preached, he moved briskly about the platform, jerking the mic cord as he went.

Then he moved to one side, getting wound up in the cord and nearly tripping before jerking it again.

After several violent circles and jerks, a little girl in the third pew leaned toward her mother and whispered, "If he gets loose, will he hurt us?"

A HAIRY SERMON

A pastor, known for his lengthy sermons, noticed a man get up and leave during the middle of his message. The man returned just before the conclusion of the service. Afterwards the pastor asked the man where he had gone.

"I went to get a haircut," was the reply.

"But," said the pastor, "why didn't you do that before the service?"

"Because," the gentleman said, "I didn't need one then."

1) Thursday night-Potluck supper. Prayer and medication to follow

2) Don't let worry kill you-let the church help.

3) A songfest was hell at the Methodist church Wednesday

4) Bertha Belch, a missionary from Africa, will be speaking tonight. You're invited to hear Bertha Belch all the way from Africa.

5) The sermon this morning: "Jesus walks on water." The sermon tonight: "Searching for Jesus."

6) Ladies don't forget the rummage sale. It's a chance to get rid of those things not worth keeping around the house. Don't forget your husbands.

7) The peacemaking meeting scheduled for today has been canceled due to a conflict.

8) The Low Self Esteem Support Group will meet Thursday at 7pm. Please use the back door.

9) Weight Watchers will meet at 7pm at the First Presbyterian Church. Please use the large double door at the side entrance

10) The associate Minister has unveiled the churches new tithing campaign slogan Sunday. It is: "I upped my pledge, now, up yours."

10 LINES TO MAKE YOU SMILE

1) My husband and I divorced over religious dif-
   ferences. He thought he was God and I didn't.
2) I used to have a handle on life, but it broke.
3) Ham and eggs. A day's work for a chicken, a
   lifetime commitment for a pig.
4) God must love stupid people. He made so
   many of them.
5) I smile because I don't know what the heck is
   going on.
6) Being "over the hill" is better than being under
   it.
7) Don't take life too seriously; no one gets out
   alive.
8) I'm not a complete idiot; some parts are miss-
   ing.
9) The gene pool could use a little chlorine.
10) Wrinkled was not one of the things I wanted
    to be when I grew up.

HAPPY ANNIVERSARY

At All Saints Lutheran Church in Morris, Minnesota they have a weekly husband's marriage seminar. At a recent session the pastor asked Ole, who was approaching his 50th wedding anniversary to take a few minutes to share some insight on 50 years of marriage to Lina.

"Vell," Ole replied to the assembled husbands', "I tried to treat her nice, spend da money on her, but best of all I took her to Norvay for da 20th anniversary."

The pastor responded, "Ole you are an amazing inspiration to all the husbands here. Please tell us what you are planning for your wife on for your 50th anniversary."

Ole proudly replied, "I'm gonna go get her."

FROM THE
MOUTHS
OF KIDS

OUCH

After the church service a little boy told the pastor, "When I grow up, I'm gonna give you some money."

"Well, thank you," the pastor replied, "But why?"

"Because my daddy say you're one of the poorest preachers we've ever had."

LESSON LEARNED

A Sunday school teacher asked her little children, as they were on their way to a church service, "And why is it necessary to be quiet in church?"

One bright little girl replied, "Because people are sleeping."

OUR FATHER

A Sunday school teacher began her lesson with a question. "Boys and girls, what do we know about God?"

A hand shot up in the air. "He is an artist," said the kindergarten boy.

"Really?! How do you know?" the teacher asked.

"You know-Our Father who does art in heaven."

RIGHT TO THE POINT

A little girl became restless as the preacher's sermon dragged on and on. Finally she leaned over to her mother and whispered, "Mommy, if we give him the money now, will he let us go?"

PINT SIZED PASTOR

After a church service on Sunday morning, a young boy suddenly announced to his mother, "Mom, I've decided to become a minister when I grow up."

"That's okay with us, but what made you decide that?"

"Well, I'll have to go to church on Sunday anyway, and I figure it will be more fun to stand and yell than to sit and listen!"

A NEW LEAF

A little boy opened the family Bible. He was fascinated as he fingered through the old pages. Suddenly, something fell out of the Bible. He picked up the object and looked closely at it. What he saw was an old leaf that had been pressed between the pages of the Good Book. "Mama, look what I found", the boy called out. "What have you got there, dear?" With astonishment in the young boy's voice, he answered, "I think it's Adam's underwear!"

AFRAID OF THE DARK

A little boy was afraid of the dark. One night his mother told him to go out on the back porch and bring her the broom. The little boy turned to his mother and said, "Mama, I don't want to go out there. It's dark." "You don't have to be afraid of the dark," she explained. "Jesus is out there. He'll look after you and protect you." The little boy looked at his mother real hard and asked, "Are you sure he's out there?" "Yes, I am sure. He is everywhere, and he is always ready to help you when you need Him," she said. The little boy thought about that for a minute and then went to the back door and cracked it a little. Peering out into the darkness he called, "Jesus, if you're out there, would you please hand me the broom?"

LESSON LEARNED

A young boy had just gotten his driving permit. He asked his father, who was a minister, if they could discuss the use of the car. His father took him to his study and said to him, "I'll make a deal with you. You bring your grades up, study your Bible and get your hair cut and we'll talk about it." After about a month the boy came back again and asked the father if they could, again, talk about the use of the car. The fathers said, "Son, I'm proud of you. You got your grades up, studied the Bible but you didn't get your haircut." The young man waited a moment and replied, "You know dad, I've been thinking about that. You know Samson had long hair, Moses had long hair, Noah had long hair and even Jesus had long hair." To which his father replied, "Yes, you're right, and they also WALKED everywhere they went!"

A CHILD IS THE TEACHER

A young woman teacher with obvious liberal tendencies explains to her class of small children that she is an atheist. She asks her class if they are atheists too. Not really knowing what atheism is, but wanting to be like their teacher, their hands exploded into the air. There is, however, one exception. A girl named Lucy has not gone along with the crowd. The teacher asks her why she has chosen to be different. "Because I am not an atheist." "Then," asks the teacher, "What are you?" "I am a Christian." The teacher is a little perturbed now, her face slightly red. She asks Lucy why she is a Christian. "Well, I was brought up knowing and loving Jesus. My mom is a Christian and my dad is a Christian, so I am a Christian." The teacher is angry now. "That's no reason." She says loudly. "What if your mom was a moron, and your dad was a moron. What would you be then?" A pause and a smile. "Then," says Lucy, "I would be an atheist."

LUNCH TIME LESSON

The Kids were lined up in the cafeteria of a Catholic elementary school for lunch. At the head of the table was a large pile of apples. A nun made a note and posted it on the apple tray.

"Take only one. God is watching."

Moving further along the lunch line sat a tray of chocolate chip cookies. A child had written a note.

"Take all you want. God is watching the apples."

A WHALE OF A STORY

A little girl was talking to her teacher about whales. The teacher said it was physically impossible for a whale to swallow a human because even though it is a very large mammal, it has a very small throat.

The little girl stated that a whale swallowed Jonah.

Irritated, the teacher reiterated that a whale could not swallow a human; it was physically impossible.

The little girl said, "When I get to heaven, I'll ask Jonah."

The teacher asked, "What if Jonah went to hell?"

The little girl replied, "Then you ask him."

KIDS EXPLAIN LOVE
(LOVE AT RESTAURANT)

"Just see if the man picks up the check. That's how you can tell if he's in love."

–Bobby age 9

"Lovers will just be staring at each other and the food gets cold. Other people care more about the food."

–Bart age 9

"See if the man had lipstick on his face."

–Sandra age 7

WHAT PEOPLE THINK WHEN THEY SAY
I LOVE YOU

"The person is thinking: Yea, I really do love him. But I hope he showers at least once a day."

–Michelle age 9

"Some lovers might be real nervous, so they are glad that they finally got it out and said it. Now they can go eat."

–Dick age 7

WHY LOVE HAPPENS

"One of the people has freckles, and so he finds somebody else who has freckles too."

–Andrew age 6

"No one is sure why it happens, but I heard it has something to do with how you smell. That's why perfume and deodorant are so popular."

–Mae age 9

WHAT'S IT LIKE TO FALL IN LOVE?

"Like an avalanche where you have to run for your life."

–John age 9

"If falling in love is anything like learning how to spell, I don't want to do it. It takes too long."

–Glenn age 7

HOW DO YOU MAKE SOMEONE
FALL IN LOVE WITH YOU?

"Tell them that you own a whole bunch of candy." stores."

–Del age 6

"One way is to take the girl out to eat. Make sure it's something she likes to eat. French fries usually work for me."

–Bart age 9

"Shake your hips and hope for the best."
–Camille age 9

WHY DO LOVERS HOLD HANDS?

"They want to make sure their rings don't fall off because they paid good money for them."

–Gavin age 8

"They are just practicing for when they march down the aisle someday and do that matchimony thing."

–John age 9

HOW IMPORTANT IS LOVE?

"Love is the most important thing in the world, but baseball is pretty good too."

—Greg age 8

After being interviewed by the school administration, the eager teaching prospect said:

"Let me see if I've got this right. You want me to go into that room with all those kids and fill their every waking moment with a love for learning? I'm supposed to instill a sense of pride in their ethnicity, modify their disruptive behavior, observe them for signs of abuse and even censor their t-shirt messages and dress habits. You want me to wage a war on drugs, check their backpacks for weapons of mass destruction, and raise their self esteem?"

"You want me to teach them patriotism, good citizenship, sportsmanship, fair play, how to register to vote, how to balance a checkbook and how to apply for a job? I am to check their heads for lice, recognize signs of anti-social behavior, encourage respect for the cultural diversity of others, and oh, make sure that I give the girls in my class 50% of my attention?"

"My contract requires me to work on my own time after school. Grade papers on evenings, weekends and vacation at my own expense. Work toward advance certification and a Masters Degree? And on my own time you want me to attend committee and faculty meetings, PTA meetings, and participate in staff development training?"

"I am to be a paragon of virtue, larger than life, such that my very presence will awe my students into being obedient and respectful of authority. You want me to incorporate technology into the learning experience, monitor web sites, and relate personally with each student? That includes deciding who might be potentially dangerous and/or liable to commit a crime in school. Plus, I am to make sure that all of the students with handicaps get an equal education regardless of the extent of their mental or physical handicap."

"And I am to communicate regularly with the parents by letter, telephone, newsletter and report card. All of this and I am to do this with a piece of paper and chalk, a computer, a few books, a bulletin board, a big smile AND on a starting salary that qualifies me and my family for food stamps?"

"You want me to do all this and you expect me…NOT TO PRAY?!?!"

Breinigsville, PA USA
09 February 2011
255217BV00001B/5/P